# Bitsy Bee Goes to SCHOOL

## by David A. Carter

Ready-to-Read

Simon Spotlight
New York London Toronto Sydney New Delhi

SIMON SPOTLIGHT

An imprint of Simon & Schuster Children's Publishing Division

1230 Avenue of the Americas, New York, New York 10020

Copyright © 2014 by David A. Carter

All rights reserved, including the right of reproduction in whole or in part in any form.

SIMON SPOTLIGHT, READY-TO-READ, and colophon are registered trademarks of Simon & Schuster, Inc.

For information about special discounts for bulk purchases, please contact Simon & Schuster Special Sales

at 1-866-506-1949 or business@simonandschuster.com.

The Simon & Schuster Speakers Bureau can bring authors to your live event. For more information or to book

an event contact the Simon & Schuster Speakers Bureau at 1-866-248-3049 or visit our website at www.simonspeakers.com.

Manufactured in the United States of America 0614 LAK

First Edition

10 9 8 7 6 5 4 3 2 1

Library of Congress Cataloging-in-Publication Data

Carter, David A., author, illustrator

Bitsy bee goes to school / by David A. Carter. -- First edition.

pages cm. -- (Ready-to-read)

Pop-up books--Specimens. I. Title.

PZ7.C2429Bk 2014 [E]--dc23

2013041407

ISBN 978-1-4424-9503-6 (pbk)

ISBN 978-1-4424-9504-3 (hc)

ISBN 978-1-4424-9505-0 (eBook)

Rise and shine!
It is the first day
of school!

Bitsy Bee looks
at her Clock Bug
and lets out a yawn.

She is excited
for school now that
summer is gone!

Mama Bug packs Bitsy
a Sandwich Bug,
along with a special treat.

Then she gives Bitsy
a big bug hug and says,
"Oh, the new Bugs
you will meet!"

Bitsy rides her
bicycle to her
brand-new bus stop.

On the bus she meets
Busy Bug,
who sits with a plop!

"What is wrong, Busy Bug?"
Bitsy asks with a frown.

"We have never been
to school," says Busy Bug
as they pass through town.

Bitsy tells Busy
not to worry.
It will be fun!

They will make new friends
and learn to count
to one hundred and one!

Busy Bug smiles.
Then the two bugs
go in to their new school.

Teacher Bug is waiting.
She says, "Welcome, Bugs.
Having fun is the first rule!"

First the Bugs
learn their ABCs.

They are led by
Alphabet Bugs called
the Spelling Bees!

Then it is time for
art class,
with Paintbrush Bugs
from red to green.

Busy Bug paints
a picture of himself
with Bitsy
in a sunset scene!

At recess,
new friends decide to
play a game.

With a Baseball Bug
and a bat,
Bitsy has great aim!

Finally the day
is over and school is
let out.

Bitsy and Busy
wave to their friends.
"See you tomorrow!"
they shout.

Hooray for a fun day
at school!